Arthur Starter Book 12

ARTHUR'S
Off to School

by Marc Brown

Long tail Books

BIONIC BUNNY
ALIENS

“Wake up, Arthur,” said D.W. “Time for school.”

Arthur groaned.

“ARTHUR, YOU’RE GOING TO BE LATE!” his mother shouted from downstairs.

“Rrrrfff! Rrrrfff!” barked Pal. Arthur tumbled out of bed.

Arthur took a big stretch. D.W. stretched, too.
Arthur went into the bathroom to wash up. D.W. followed him.

Arthur ate his cereal in a hurry. So did D.W.

"Stop copying me!" said Arthur.

"I'm practicing for next year," explained D.W., "when I go to school."

"That's silly," said Arthur.

"Is not," D.W. insisted.

"Oh, yeah?" said Arthur. "Well, can you copy this?"

He grabbed his backpack and rushed out the door.

The Brain didn't have a sister to bother him. But he did have another problem. "Here, lizard!" he called out. "Here, lizard, lizard . . ."

SCIENCE
MATH
SCIENCE
CHEMISTRY

STOP

Binky wasn't worried about little sisters or lost pets.
He was worried about looking tough.
"I do have my reputation to keep up," he thought.

1ST PRIZE
ELIZA
GO LAKEWOOD!
1ST

Francine had troubles, too.
"I have to be ready for recess," she said.
"You never know what you might need."

Muffy wasn't looking that far ahead.
"What to wear?" she asked herself.
"Maybe something pink. I look so cute in pink."

Buster didn't have any problems at all. But his mother did.
"Buster!" she shouted. "Wake up!"

USA
BIONIC BUNNY

Arthur met his friends in class.
"I wonder what Mr. Ratburn is planning for today," said the Brain.
"Maybe a field trip," said Binky.
"A sports field trip," added Francine.

"Oh, no!" said Muffy. "My outfit's all wrong for that."
"Whatever happened to nap time?" asked Buster.
Arthur shrugged. "I don't care what it is," he said, "as long as it's away from D.W."

The bell rang. “Hand in your homework, everyone!” said Mr. Ratburn.
Suddenly, Arthur remembered something.
His homework was sitting on the kitchen table.
Mr. Ratburn cleared his throat. *I’m doomed*, thought Arthur.

6 x 6 =
3 x 9 =
5 x 3 =

FISH
SOLAR SYSTEM
6 ×
3 ×
5 ×

Then he heard a knock at the door. D.W. was standing there with Dad.
"Homework delivery!" she announced.
Arthur rushed up to her. "I'm still practicing," she whispered.
"Thanks," he whispered back.

Arthur had to admit it. Sometimes little sisters were a big pain, but sometimes they were a big help, too.